POW

CREATED AND PRODUCED
BY
RIAN MICHAEL BENDIS
AND
MIKE AVON OEMING

ERS

COLOR ART
PETER PANTAZIS

TYPOGRAPHY
KEN BRUZENAK

EDITORS
KC MCCRORY AND **JAMIE S. RICH**
WITH **JAMES LUCAS JONES**

BUSINESS AFFAIRS
ALISA BENDIS

DESIGN ASSISTANCE
KEITH WOOD

Previously in Powers

Detectives Christian Walker and Deena Pilgrim
work out of the special homicide unit in charge
of cases that involve Powers.

Walker has been off the force for almost a year
due to his scandalous interview in the press about
the federal corruption in law enforcement.

The Dawn of Man

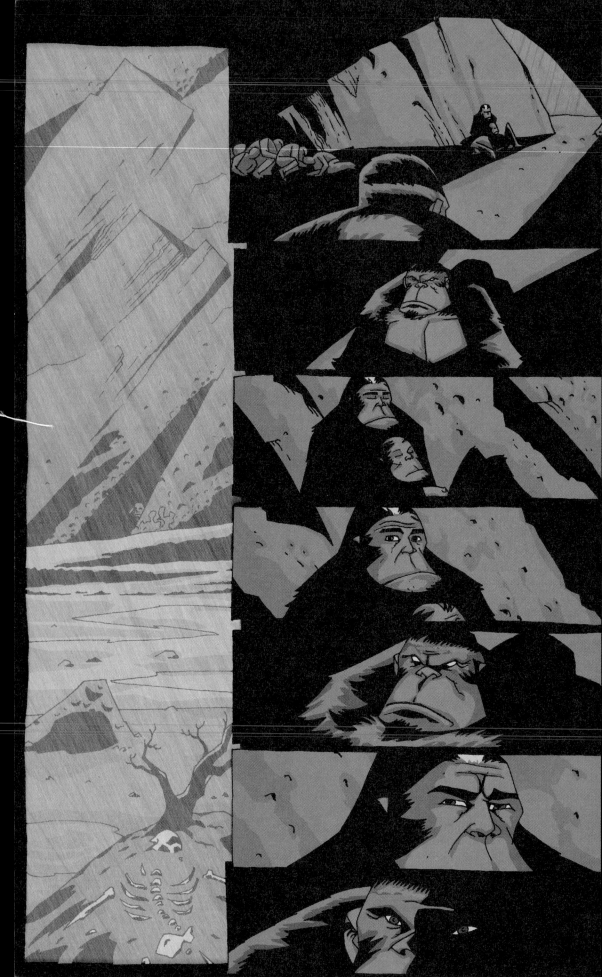

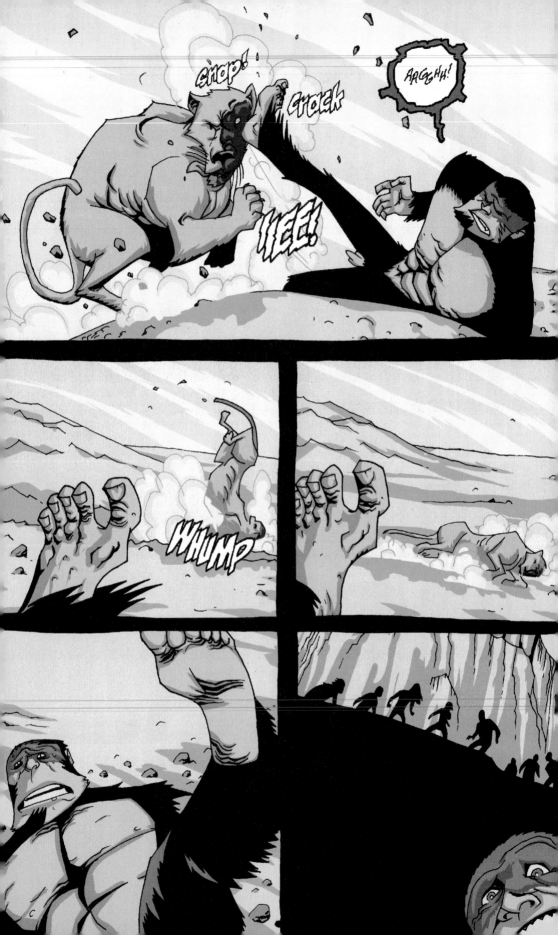

GPRRR PRRRR...

GGFSKK!

GROBONKL!

FRUNK!

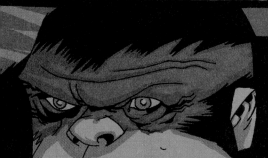

SPLUMK!

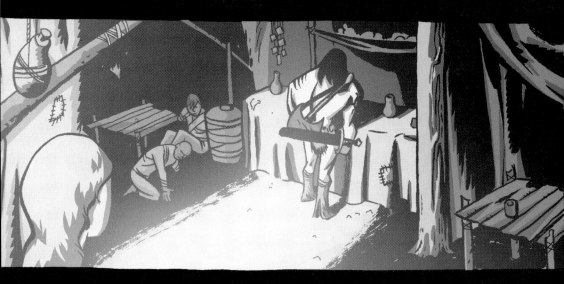

A STRANGER. I NEED A BED TO SLEEP.

WHERE DO YOU HAIL FROM?

JUST A BED. AND A BATH.

FOR HOW LONG? THE NIGHT? THE SEASON?

I DON'T KNOW. SIX DAYS.

I NEED PAYMENT UP FRONT.

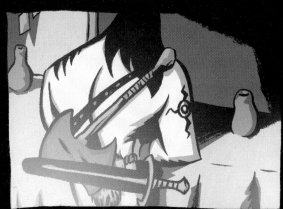

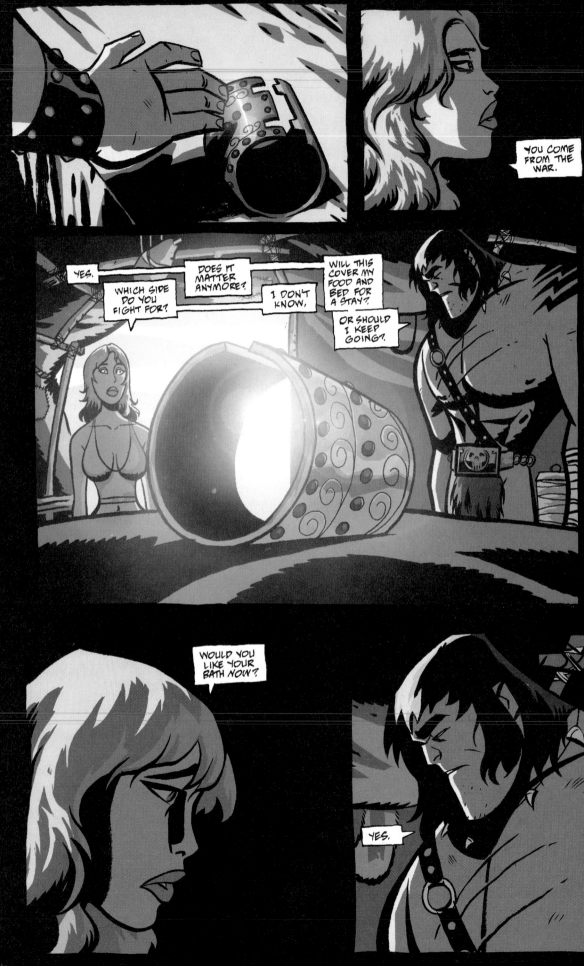

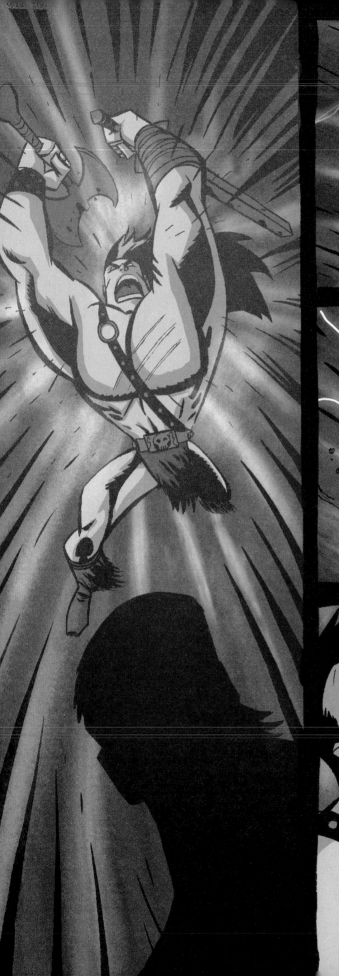

HYAARGGH!

THAT IS IT! SEE?

YOUR TRUE POW YOU CAN'T CONT IT, CAN YOU, Y CAN'T HOLD IT

CHACK!

WOSHU
MOUNTAIN
TEMPLE

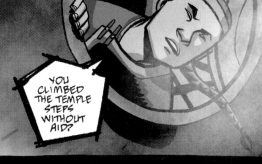

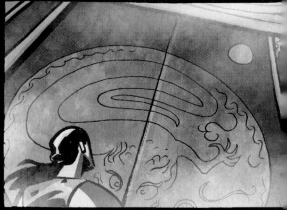

16 YEARS LATER

WAIT, HO—WE HAVE A VISITOR.

WHERE?

AMAZING.

WHO IS IT?

A MAN~ FROM THE CITY, A DOCTOR.

HE CLIMBED THE STEPS HIMSELF?

HE LAY AT THE DOOR LIKE THIS. HE IS IN A BAD WAY.

I DON'T KNOW HOW LONG.

WHAT BRINGS YOU HERE?

MY NAME IS WONG.

I·I·I·I COME FROM THE CITY OF PEKING.

I·I·I COME HERE WITH HUMILITY. I COME TO YOU FOR WISDOM, AND PITY.

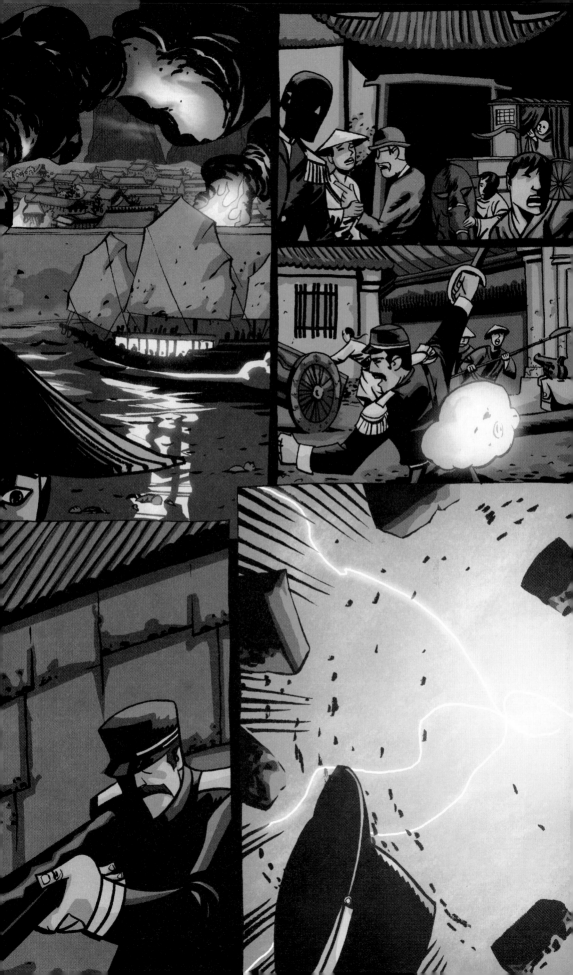

MYSTERY MAN
TAKES ON THE M

Gangland Quakes at Assault on Unde

Police Baffled, But Vow Arrest Comin

ARTIST RENDERING OF MYSTERY VIGILANTE

Have you seen this man? Police are beating the bushes from the Stockyards to the Loop trying to bring him in for "questioning."

POLICE COMMISSIONER "Irish Red" O'Malley lashed out once again at the mysterious crimefighter that has has been making a fool of the city's Boys in Blue.

Refusing questions from reporters from the Herald-Examiner, O'Malley launched into a ten-minute tirade against the new "crimebuster" who seems to be doing the job the cops can't handle. Clearly embarassed by the success of his competitor in mopping up mob activity, O'Malley attempted several times to paint his nemesis as just another hood, but John Q. Public isn't buying it. Reporters and passers-by at City Hall clearly booed down the Commissioner's bluster, and loudly cheered every time Chicago's newest crusader against crime was mentioned.

Clearly frustrated, O'Malley stormed off the stage, swearing

(continued on page A2)

Eins
Visit

Professor Al
town
distinguis
nation's br
"Special T
This countr
been trying
make use of

*"It's v
explain, a
to apply, b*

work for years
brilliant scien
new light
everyday usea
Theory."
Some of the

(co

SKULL TAKER LAY

THIS IS A *TRICK*?

YOU MUST BE A TRICK.

NO.

HOW COULD— HOW *COULD* I EVEN...?

VHAT ELSE? SHOW ME MORE!!

"NITTI RUNS THE CHICAGO MOB.

HIS GUYS, THEY BROKE MY WIFE'S BROTHER'S LEGS BECAUSE HE OWES THEM MONEY.

HE PLAYS THE PONIES-- NOT REALLY *WELL*, I GATHER, FROM THE WAY IT'S ALL TURNED OUT.

"ANYWAY, I--I *HAD* TO DO SOMETHING.

THESE RAT BASTARDS, I HAD TO.

"THEY GOT THE COPS IN THEIR POCKETS, THE MAYOR.

"IT'S BEEN GOING ON FOR *YEARS* AND *YEARS*. NO ONE'S DOING ANYTHING, NO ONE *WILL* DO ANYTHING.

"SO IT'S EITHER *ME* OR NOTHING.

"BUT ALL THE SAME, I DIDN'T WANT ANYONE *KNOWING* IT WAS ME.

"I DIDN'T WANT TO PUT MY WIFE IN ANY KIND OF DANGER OR NOTHIN'.

"I JUST WANTED TO GET IN AND OUT AND TEACH THEM... TEACH THEM *SOMETHING*...I JUST WANTED THEM TO *STOP*.

"SO I PUT ON THE MASK.

"I KNOW IT'S SOME SILLY...JUST A MASK. A HALLOWEEN MASK.

"BUT IT'S ALL I COULD THINK OF, SO I PUT IT ON."

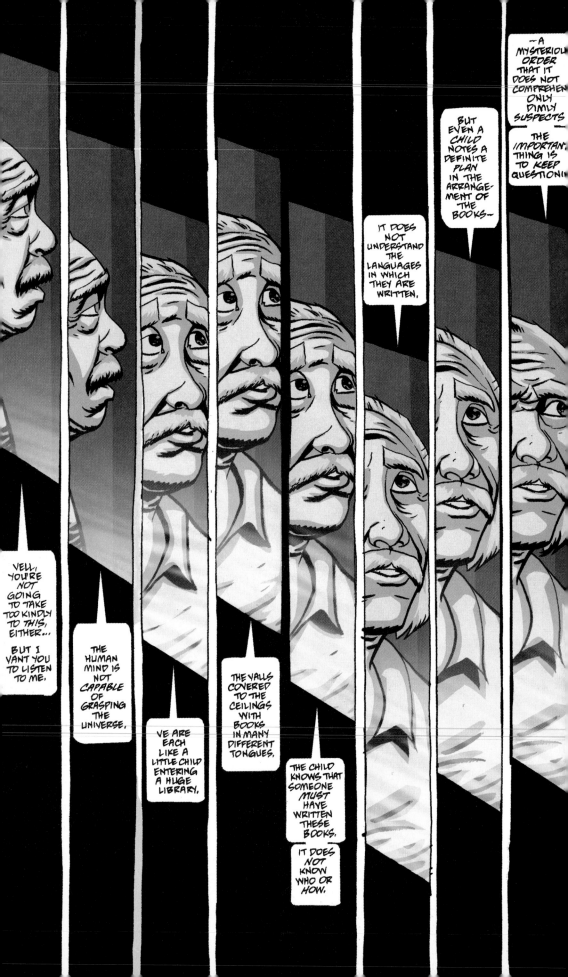

GOING THROUGH THE RETRO GIRL PHOTO FILE AGAIN.

LOOKING TO SEE IF ANYONE KEEPS POPPING UP IN THE BACKGROUND, Y'KNOW?

THE CASE IS CLOSED.

NOT TO MY SATISFACTION.

IT'S CLOSED. IT'S DONE.

IT'S DONE.

THING IS, MAN, I DIDN'T EVEN KNOW HER AND I THINK THIS CASE ENDED SHIT.

YOU KNEW HER, AND--

--YOU KNEW HER, AND YOU'RE ALL--

IT'S DONE.

IT WAS YOUR FIRST CASE. FIRST CASES ALWAYS EAT AT YOU.

DON'T KNOW WHY, THEY JUST DO. IT'S DONE.

AND NOTHING ABOUT THIS IS STICKING IN YOUR GUT, LIKE--

IT'S A FEELING YOU GET USED TO.

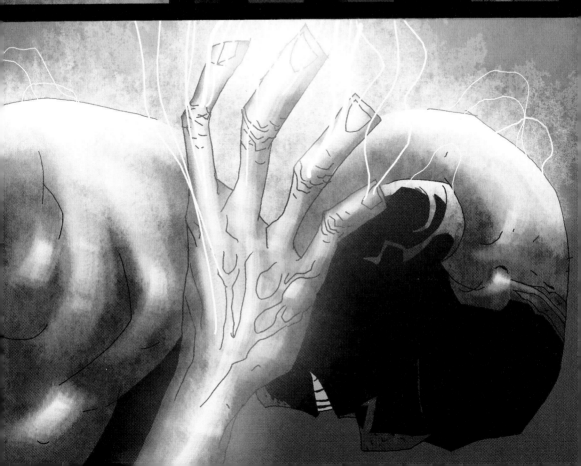

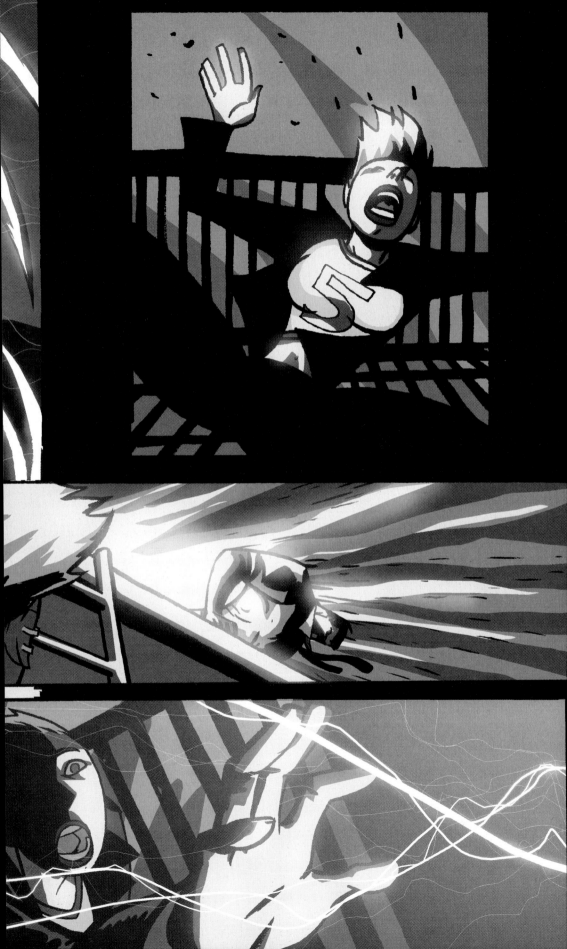

THE SCRIPT

Ah. The infamous monkey issue.

I think the phone call I made to Mike Oeming after writing this issue was: "Hey, Mike, I think I just killed our book. This might be the beginning of the end."

Yeah, yeah. We had this grand vision for this giant mythological story of ours and we knew this is how we wanted to open the story. With a big fucking nod to Stanley Kubrick and a real in your face "we're not fucking around with this" attitude, but we also knew that a lot of people buy this comic for some superhero homicide detective fiction and this ain't that.

And its one thing to think about writing something like this, it's another thing to have done it and realize how whacked out this might seem at first. See you guys got to read this story in one sitting, the monthly POWERS readers had to wait six weeks to get a clue to what was actually happening.

But we had a story to tell and a way we wanted to tell it, so we bit our lip and got on with it.

But, boy, I didn't think I was going to be getting monkey fucker jokes via email to this DAY. Alright already! I've heard them!

You should have seen my AOL account the first two months after this issue shipped. Every subject header was:

MONKEY FUCKER
MONKEY ASS
MONKEY TAINT
MONKEY CUM
MONKEY ANAL
MONKEY LOVE WITH HOWARD STERN
MONKEY SMEGMA

And on and on it went. I am sure my account got flagged. It looked like I was running some kind of monkey porn ring or something.

But gratefully most everyone hung in with the book and got into the ride, but because this issue was so closely scrutinized and because now that you've read the entire story you might appreciate what went into this on another level, or just to show you that, yes, I actually wrote a script for this issue, we are presenting the full script to issue 31.

The monkey fucker issue.

Enjoy.

Or whatever.

POWERS
BY BRIAN MICHAEL BENDIS
AND MICHAEL AVON OEMING
ISSUE THIRTY ONE
FOREVER MAN PART ONE

Ok. So...

This story arc is about the first two superheroes ever.

And they are reincarnated souls whose grudge match battle to the death takes centuries and centuries. One of them will know they are reincarnated and the other will not.

Each chapter will take place in a different time period. With different feelings and tones to them.

This first chapter is the dawn of man. Please reference the opening of 2001 for tone and look. This is a direct, bold homage to that part of the film but we will gradually build on it.

The ape man figures are really dense black fur figures against the bland, bleached out, minimal backgrounds.

The color tone is oranges. Monochromatic.

The font clearly identifies to the reader that vocalizing hurts. As if the vocal chords aren't fully formed.

Page 1-

Full page image

Wide shot of a desolate, almost desert plane, a couple of badly formed hills and mountains. No greenery. No brush. Just the earth in its earliest days.

The hazy sun is setting in the distance miles away.

White Times Roman Type reads: The dawn of man.

Page 2- 3

Double page spread

Another incredibly wide shot of the desolate desert earth. As if the camera in page one, shifted over to the right to show even more of this incredibly desolate world.

But in the middle of page 3 a half dozen ape men are hovering around a water hole.

For reference- here is some of my research on this that I think will help your artwork.

About 3 million year ago, the earth was populated with deer, giraffes, hyenas, cattle, sheep, goats, antelope, gazelles, horses, elephants, rhinoceroses, camels, ground squirrels, beavers, cave lions, ants, termites, porpoises, whales, dogs with huge teeth, and sabre-toothed tigers! Giant sharks, about 42 feet long, were plentiful.

There were all kinds of birds and plants and fish, similar to birds, plants and fish today. (Dinosaurs died out about 65 million years ago. They were long gone.)

About this Same time in history, around 3 million years ago, the higher primates, including apes and early man, first appeared. There was a difference between

the apes and man. Human-like hominids could stand upright. Apes could not. Their hands were different, too. Ape hands were made for climbing and clinging.

Early man's hands were jointed differently, which allowed them to not only use tools, but to make tools. No one knows if they actually made tools, but remains of polished bones have been found in South Africa, which suggests they might have made simple digging tools from bone!

Their diet was mostly vegetarian, along with some meat, probably obtained by scavenging.

Page 4-

1- Mid shot of the six ape man hovering around the shallow watering hole. Drinking water out of their hands or putting their lips lightly to the water.

In the foreground, a small dead reptilian animal behind them they killed and ate a reptile and are now drinking. There are also some berry branches stripped of their fruit.

The man-apes were starving to death. What little food they could find consisted of only a few bugs, roots and if they were lucky enough to find one before the tapirs got to it, maybe a grub or two.

Obviously they are on the brink of extinction as evidenced by the "humanoid" bones lying around We are beginning to see slight difference in the apemen.

One is a woman. And two are a bit larger that all the rest.

Of the larger, one has a white shock in his hair like the bride of Frankenstein. He is White Stripe.

The other is a bit larger than the all the others and he has a big Red Stripe across his eyes and back. Almost like a mask.

The other three are normal black furry ape men with no features.

2- White Stripe lifts his face from the water. He has a content look on his face. He is a peaceful soul.

WHITE STRIPE
Ggrrrpprrr...

3- The woman ape lazily drips water on her chest without realizing anyone cares. Seduction.

WOMAN APE
Gggsskkk!!

4- Red Stripe watches The woman ape and honks his approval.

RED STRIPE

Groonkkkhh1!

5- The woman ape glares at Red Stripe with contempt.

WOMAN APE
Fftt!

6- Red Stripe grimaces at the insult.

RED STRIPE
Snort!

7- From behind Red Stripe, The woman turns away and goes back to the water. She is ignoring him.

Page 5-

1- Red Stripe gives her a glaringly evil look.

2- From behind the White Stripe. White Stripe watches her quietly as she drinks. In the background, Red Stripe watches the two of them.

3- The woman honks approvingly at White Stripe as water dribbles from her mouth.

WOMAN APE
Hoffkk!!

4- White Stripe honks back. They are flirting.

WHITE STRIPE
Ghhonkkk!!

5- The woman sticks her little ass in the air as she goes back to drinking.

6- White Stripe looks at her ass sticking up. He is feeling randy.

7- White Stripe's p.o.v. Tight on the ass.

8- Tighter on White Stripe looking at the ass longingly.

Page 6-

1- From behind Red Stripe, White Stripe mounts the woman and starts going at it.

> WHITE STRIPE
> Gruunk!

> WOMAN
> Hugh!

> WHITE STRIPE
> Gruunk!

2- The Red Stripe watches this from across the small pond, he ain't happy.

> WHITE STRIPE
> Gruunk!
> WOMAN
> Hugh!

> WHITE STRIPE
> Gruunk!

3- The two go at it. They do not notice Red Stripe.

> WHITE STRIPE
> Gruunk!

> WOMAN
> Hugh!

> WHITE STRIPE
> Gruunk!

4- The woman drinks as he humps her.

> WHITE STRIPE
> Gruunk!

> WOMAN
> Hugh!

> WHITE STRIPE
> Gruunk!

5- The other apes seem agitated and excited. One starts to whack it and doesn't even know why.

> WHITE STRIPE
> Gruunk!

> WOMAN
> Hugh!

> WHITE STRIPE
> Gruunk!

> APE
> Gahh!!

> APE
> Faap!!

> APE
> Gfaapp!!

> APE
> Raaffggh!

Page 7-

1- White Stripe barks at the sky. His entire face curled into a childlike smile of glee. He is finishing.

> WHITE STRIPE
> Hhaarrgghh!!

2- From behind the Red Stripe, White Stripe keeps fucking the woman and barks back.

> WHITE STRIPE
> Yyaarrggff!!!

> WOMAN
> Hagh huagh huagh

> WHITE STRIPE
> Yyaarrggff!!!

> WOMAN
> Hagh huagh huagh

> WHITE STRIPE
> Yyaarrggff!!!

3- Tight on the woman panting into the water, water dripping from her mouth.

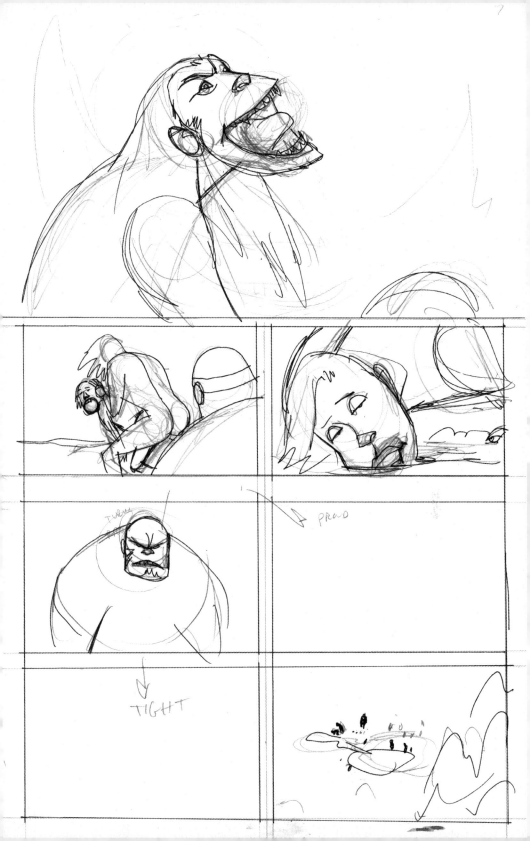

PROD

TIGHT

WOMAN
Hagh huagh huagh

4- Red Stripe glares at the scene.

RED STRIPE
Hoggnnk!

5- White Stripe looks at Red Stripe for the first time since the act began.

Its a satisfied look that is being mistaken for an arrogant look of conquest.

6- Same as 4, but tighter.

7- Mid wide of the small pond. Red Stripe is walking away as the rest continue to drink.

Page 8-

1- Ext. Cave- night

Its a crevice inside a badly formed mountain side in this barren wasteland. The crevice is a crooked, slanted triangle if an opening.

It is pouring. A monstrous amount of night rain.

2- Int. Cave- Same

The apes all sleep up against the wall of the cave. White Stripe sleeping next to woman ape. All the other apes asleep on her other side. White Stripe sleeping closest to the cave opening. Everyone huddled.

3- Sitting across from the rest of the apes is the Red Stripe. He is sitting and hugging himself. He is wide awake, staring at the White Stripe.

4- Red Stripe's p.o.v. The White Stripe is sleeping.

5- Same, The White Stripe opens his eyes and looks at the Red Stripe sitting across from him.

6- Tight on the Red Stripe staring back.

7- Same as 4,

8- Same as 5.

Page 9-

1- Ext. Desert- day

Big panel. Action!

The man-apes are running towards us in a furious panic. They are being attacked by a hungry leopard who is nipping at their heels. Everyone is running away from the leopard with a panic and desperation.

They are running across a mostly open desert plane. Mountains behind them. a young tree here and there. Nothing to climb up.

This day is very blanche. Almost yellow, white, hot. Sunny but hazy.

WOMAN
Gyyaaarrgghhh!!!

2- White Stripe is running and looking around in a panic for somewhere to hide.

WHITE STRIPE
Huf hufgh hufgh!!

3- White Stripe finds a steep cliff to scamper up in the distance and yells for everyone to follow him.

WHITE STRIPE
Hugh Hyaauugghh!!

4- Profile, silhouette of the incline. The others follow his lead as the leopard is just about to get to them.

5- The woman ape is climbing and crying, she looks back at...

WOMAN APE
Hyyiii!!

6- Woman ape's p.o.v. High looking down. The leopard barks and leaps. He can't follow them up the incline.

LEOPARD
Rrraagghhrr!!

Page 10-

1- The Red Stripe climbs up past White Stripe. Both are stronger and climb much faster than the others.

WHITE STRIPE
Huh huh huh!!!

2- Wide of the incline hillside. All the apes are scampering. The leopard can't reach them.

                    APE
        Ffttt!!

                    APE
        ggaap!!

                    APE
        aapp!!

                    APE
        Raaffggh!

3- The White Stripe reaches down to pull the woman ape up.

                WHITE STRIPE
        Gruunk!

                    WOMAN
        Hugh!

4- High looking down. The leopard leers quiet, menacing, looking for his chance.

5- Low looking up. Past the leopard looking up at The apes mocking him. Hanging off the rocks and mocking him. The littlest apes closest to the leopard.

                WHITE STRIPE
        Gruunk!

                    WOMAN
        Hugh!

                WHITE STRIPE
        Gruunk!

                    APE
        Gahh!!

                    APE
        Faap!!

                    APE
        Gfaapp!!

                    APE
        Raaffggh!

6- High looking down, The leopard jumps.

                    LEOPARD
        Aarrgghh!!

Page 11-

1- Profile. The leopard leaps and grabs one of the smaller apes by the foot. Pulling him down.

                    APE
        Aaiiiasaaee!!
2- Low looking up. The other apes all react in shock and climb higher.

                WHITE STRIPE
        Aaeegghhk!

                    WOMAN
        Hugh!

                WHITE STRIPE
        Aakktt!

                    APE
        Gahh!!

                    APE
        Eeeaaa!!

3- The leopard viciously eats the young ape alive. Holding him down on the ground firmly with a paw to the chest and is Tearing him up.

                    APE
        Aaaaiirrgghhaarrgghh!!

4- The Red Stripe, panicked, wide eyed, grabs a rock off the ledge.

                    APE
                (off panel)
        Aaaiiee!!!

5- The Red Stripe throws the rock down to the ground.

                RED STRIPE
        Hurugh!!

6- High looking down. The rock misses and bounces as the leopard continues to eat the ape, now dead.

                    LEOPARD
        Ggggg....

Spx: thump

7- The Red Stripe grabs another rock, this time determined to do something.

8- The Red Stripe throws the rock down to the ground.

> RED STRIPE
> Hurugh!!

Page 12-

1- Mid shot of the leopard. The rock bashes him on the head.

Spx: bonk

> LEOPARD
> Aeeiii

2- The woman and the White Stripe watching this.

3- The leopard is hurt. Dazed and bleeding from the head.

4- The White Stripe also grabs a rock and throws it too.

5- The new rock hits the leopard. The leopard has killed his little ape.

Spx: bonk

> LEOPARD
> Aeeiii

6- The Red Stripe digs at the ledge to grab a big rock...

Page 13-

1- Mid wide, full figure, profile.

Red Stripe slips off the ledge trying to throw it. He is

falling backwards, totally shocked and confused by his predicament.

> RED STRIPE
> Yip!!

2- From behind the Red Stripe, Red Stripe falls on his back right in front of the bleeding leopard.

Spx: whump

> RED STRIPE
> Ooff!!

3- The Red Stripe's p.o.v. The leopard immediately turns and hunches, ready to pounce.

4- Red Stripe gets a hold of himself, realizing what kind of deep shit he is in. He is lying right next to the bleeding, dead carcass of his little friend.

5- The leopard lunges for the kill, teeth out.

> LEOPARD
> Raaarrgghh!!

6- White Stripe and the woman ape's faces drop in horror as they watch this horrible scene.

Page 14-

1- Big panel, profile. Red Stripe, still lying on his back, kicks the leopard in the face And snaps his neck.

Spx: crack snap

> RED STRIPE
> Aagghh!!

> LEOPARD
> Iiee!!

2- The leopard falls a few feet away- its head barely hanging on. Dust billows.

Spx: whump

3- Close up on the leopard's face. Eyes open. Blood

He is Dead.

4- The Red Stripe is stunned and confused by this. Its a quiet moment after all the craziness. His foot still half up.

5- The others, still on the cliff are stunned. The smaller apes are stunned. Confused. They can't register how this worked.

Page 15-

1- The Red Stripe slowly gets up. He can't take his eyes off the dead carcass of the leopard lying in the foreground.

2- The Red Stripe yells at it.

RED STRIPE
Hyhyaaghg raarr!! ffaarrggh!!

3- Red Stripe gently, nervously approaches the dead carcass with his hand out. He wants to touch it but he is scared to.

4- Red Stripe's hand is close to touching the leopard...

5- White Stripe and the woman ape's faces are frozen with eyes wide open.

6- Red Stripe touches the carcass shoving it a little...

7- Red Stripe spills back, afraid that he has woken up the leopard.

RED STRIPE
Ffaasggh!!

8- Red Stripe's p.o.v. The leopard lies dead.

Page 16-

1- High looking down. The others start to tentatively climb down the ledge/ cliff. The leopard lies dead below them. Red Stripe still looks at it.

2- Red Stripe Looks down at his own foot with first curiosity. Considering what he did.

3- Red Stripe's p.o.v. His hairy foot.

4- Red Stripe kicks the leopard again viciously- with confidence. Its guts plop out from a superpowered force. The others bark back in shock.

RED STRIPE
Hyyaaggh!!

Spx: whump

Spx: splat

5- The others all bark back in shock.

WHITE STRIPE
Aaeegghhk!

WOMAN
Hugh!

WHITE STRIPE
Aakktt!

APE
Gahh!!

APE
Eeeaaa!!

6- Low looking up. Red Stripe howls in triumph. His new found power and confidence.

RED STRIPE
Hhaaaooooaaaaa!!!!

Page 17-

1- Ext. Pond. Dusk

Similar scene to the beginning of the issue, but the sky is almost red. There's something in the air. Its the end of the day.

Mid shot of the now five ape man hovering around the watering hole. Drinking water out of their hands or putting their lips to the water.

In the foreground, the dead leopard has been gutted and eaten raw. They ate him and are now drinking.

2- White Stripe lifts his face from the water. He has a content look on his face.

     WHITE STRIPE
    Ggrrrpprrr...

3- The woman lazily drips water on her chest without realizing anyone cares. The seduction begins again.

     WOMAN APE
    Gggsskkk!!

4- Red Stripe, with a new sense of self worth, watches and honks his approval.

     RED STRIPE
    Groonkkkhh1!

5- The woman looks back at him with a new found curiosity.

6- Red Stripe looks at her with new found assurance. He looks at her like he owns her.

     RED STRIPE
    Frunk.

7- From behind Red Stripe, The woman turns away and goes back to the water. She is ignoring him again. The White Stripe is getting ready to jump her.

8- Same as six, but tighter.

9- Tight on the Red Stripe's foot stepping forward into the water.

Spx: splumk

Page 18-

1- Red Stripe shoves White Stripe to the ground with a dismissive elbow and mounts the woman ape, to her surprise, and starts going at it.

The White Stripe has lost his footing and is shocked by this new development.

     RED STRIPE
    Gruunk!

     WOMAN APE
    Hugh!

     WHITE STRIPE
    Unk!

2- The Red Stripe really goes for it. Quick and hard.

     RED STRIPE
    Gruunk!

     WOMAN APE
    Hugh!

     RED STRIPE
    Gruunk!

3- The White Stripe scrambles to his feet and tries to stop the rape.
The other monkey's are watching this.

     WHITE STRIPE
    Gruunk!

     WOMAN
    Hugh!

     WHITE STRIPE
    Gruunk!

4- The Red Stripe, without missing a stroke, viciously back hands White Stripe.

     RED STRIPE
    Gruunk!

Spx: ftunk

     WHITE STRIPE
    Gunk!

5- White Stripe goes flying backwards into the other apes.

     WOMAN
    Hugh!

     WHITE STRIPE
    Gruunk!

      APE
    Aaaiicckk!!

      APE
    Wwaaiiggh!!

Page 19-

1- The White Stripe gets up, shocked by the violence and watching this turn of events. The other apes seem agitated and excited.

     WHITE STRIPE
    Gruunk!

APE
~~Gahh!!~~

APE
Faap!!

APE
Gfaapp!!

APE
Raaffggh!

2- From behind the White Stripe, the Red Stripe keeps his violent rape going. The woman's face is half in the water.

RED STRIPE
Gruunk!
Gruunk!
Gruunk!

WOMAN APE
Hugh!

RED STRIPE
Gruunk!
Gruunk!

3- White Stripe barks at the sky in internal pain. His entire face curled into a childlike anger.

WHITE STRIPE
Hhaarrgghh!!

4- From behind the Red Stripe, White Stripe lunges towards him.

WHITE STRIPE
Yyaarrggff!!!

RED STRIPE
Gruunk!
Gruunk!

5- The White Stripe knocks the Red Stripe off of the woman and into the water. They both tumble into the water.

RED STRIPE
~~Hoggnnk!~~

Spx: spalash

Page 20- 21

Double page spread

1- In the shallow water, the White Stripe pounds at the Red Stripe with both fists. Water splashes.

Behind them the woman rolls on the ground in pain.

RED STRIPE

Huaaggh!

WHITE STRIPE
Hugh hugh hugh!!

Spx: thump thump

2- The smaller apes jump up and down in irritation. The violence incites them.

APE
Aaagghh!!

APE
Eeeii!!

3- Profile. The Red Stripe swipes the White Stripe with a wide back arm and the White Stripe goes flying up out of the water and over the woman.
Spx: whump

4- The White Stripe lands on his face and stomach hard, stirring up dust, pebbles, and dirt from the force of the impact. Quite a few yards from the scene at the pond behind him.

Spx: thump

WHITE STRIPE
Gumph!

5- From behind the Red Stripe, The woman ape takes this moment to viciously attack the Red Stripe. She lunges and claws at his chest, crying and howling.

WOMAN APE
Aaaoohhh!! Aagghhooohhh!!

6- The Red Stripe grabs her arms and stops her attack but she is still thrashing.

WOMAN APE
Aaaoohhh!! Aagghhooohhh!!

7- From behind the Red Stripe, the woman ape is over powered by his grip but she is not giving up.

WOMAN APE
Aaaoohhh!! Aagghhooohhh!!

RED STRIPE
Huuaarrgh!

8- Same as 6, but tighter, Red Stripe yells at her to stop. His eyes turning black. Black liquid.

WOMAN APE
Aaaoohhh!!

RED STRIPE
Hhyyuuaarrgghh!!

9- Same but seven, tight on the woman apes mouth as

she screams in pain and horror at her attacker.

WOMAN APE
Aaaoohhh!! Aagghhooohhh!!

10- Same as 6, but tighter. a red swirl pours into the black liquid of his eyes.

11- Same as 9, but tighter. Her mouth goes from pain to shock, something is happening to her and her tongue sticks out a little in shock.

Page 22-23

Double page spread

1- Big panel, from behind the Red Stripe, the woman ape is melting.

She melts into thick black goo. Almost as if she is decomposing into waste. The black hair turns to tar.

Her face starts to slide off her head shape.

Her one good eye looks up in pain and sadness. She is dead.

2- The smaller apes all calm down and stare.

3- Mid shot, the Red Stripe in confused that the woman in his arms has now totally turned to liquid and is pouring through his hairy fingers.

4- Wide. The smaller apes run away as fast as they can.

Scared shitless. This tribe is officially broken up. They are running and not turning back.

The Red Stripe doesn't even notice them go.

APE
Aakk!!

APE
Eek!!

APE
Aaiiee!!

5- 3/4's view of the Red Stripe looking at his hands and the black puddle at his feet, he is confused and surprisingly calm. Melancholy.

6- Same, the camera turning slightly as he holds up one of his hands and sniffs it.

7- Same, the camera keeps turning, the Red Stripe now faces us straight, but we reveal that standing upright behind him is a pissed off and very determined White Stripe.

They will fight.

8- Tight on the White Stripe, he is stunned. Confused, his woman is gone.

9- The White Stripe's p.o.v. The Red Stripe's back. He is still hunched over the puddle of black goo, trying to figure it out.

10- Same as 8, but the White Stripe shakes off the sadness and is ready to fight.

WHITE STRIPE
Hyuunnk!

Page 24-

1- The White Stripe rushes toward the Red Stripe with intense passion to kill.

WHITE STRIPE
Hyyaarrgghh!!

2- The Red Stripe turns to face his attacker.

3- The White Stripe punches at him, more like flailing his entire arm, not a very practiced move. None of the moves here will be graceful.

WHITE STRIPE
Hyyaagghh!!

Spx: whuuummm

4- The Red Stripe catches the punch clumsily. a move that surprises them both.

Spx: smack

> RED STRIPE
> Hur!

5- The White Stripe whips around and hits him with his other arm. The Red Stripe really takes the hit.

Spx: smunk

> WHITE STRIPE
> Aarrggh!!

Page 25-

1- From behind The White Stripe, the Red Stripe is hunched over from the hit but he raises his head a bit. The Red Stripe took the punch. It didn't hurt.

2- The Red Stripe swings up and punches the White Stripe in the jaw.

Spx: smack

3- From behind The Red Stripe, The White Stripe stumbles back a step but is surprised to see he could take the punch as well.

4- The White Stripe regains his wits and hits the Red Stripe hard.

> WHITE STRIPE
> Hhaaggh!!

Spx: crack

5- Unhurt, The Red Stripe punches the White Stripe in the neck.

> RED STRIPE
> Guh!

Spx: whump

6- The Red Stripe growls at him as his eyes turns black and red again. He is using his powers to destroy his attacker.

> RED STRIPE
> Hhyyaagghhh!!

7- The White Stripe's surprised eyes burn yellow and a bubble or two pops out. The White Stripe is instinctively fighting back with his own powers.
This is officially the first superhero fight scene ever.

> WHITE STRIPE
> Hugh hugh huguh!

8- Small panel. The Red Stripe is surprised. His eyes pool back towards normal.

> RED STRIPE
> Gy?

9- Small panel. The White Stripe is confused by all of this. His eyes also pool back to normal.

> WHITE STRIPE
> Fftt.

Page 26-27

Double page spread

This is the first super powered battle.

This is a double page montage of a fight that will never end.

They are evenly matched. And evenly determined to win. Its a cave man boxing match that will never finish.

Each panel is the Same angle. Two shot, mid shot. Of the cave man hitting each other, each taking a turn, each trying to choke the other, one flipping the other. One dodging the other.

The figures are silhouette mostly. Two black figures in a violent dance. In my head they take on almost a Harvey Kurtzman fluidity. Very dramatic, expressive figure work.

To accentuate the never ending aspect each row has more and more panels. The panels getting smaller and smaller.

The first row has five widescreen panels.

The second row has seven. The third row has 9, the forth row has 11, the fifth has 11, the sixth has 13, by the time we are towards the bottom rows of the spread the panels and figures are so small that it is just stick figures hitting each other.

The background color over the piece graduates from top row to bottom row- red to orange. One gradation across the entire spread.

Page 28-

1- From behind The White Stripe, The Red Stripe with an almost sleepy exhaustion in his eyes, holds up his arm to punch down, but doesn't have the energy to keep it up.

The fight is ending.

> RED STRIPE
> Hugh...
>
> Hugh...
>
> Hugh...

2- From behind The Red Stripe, The White Stripe is equally tired but will not back down.

He sees that The Red Stripe is wavering and is curious to see what will happen next.

> WHITE STRIPE
> Hugh...
>
> Hugh...
>
> Hugh...

3- Similar to 1, The Red Stripe has no more steam, the arm is coming down.

> RED STRIPE
> Hugh...
>
> Hugh...

4- Wide of the pond area, the two of them stand feet apart, both totally exhausted.

5- Tight on the White Stripe. He is exhausted, sad and exhausted. His fur matted down by sweat. No fight left.

6- The Red Stripe looks disgusted with the whole thing,

Page 29-

Full page image

Identical to page one. But its getting dark, deep red sky.

Wide shot of a desolate, almost desert plane, a couple of badly formed hills and mountains. No greenery. No brush. Just the earth in its earliest days.

The two ape men walk away from each other in opposite directions. They are already yards away. Both hunched over and exhausted. The fight over... For now.

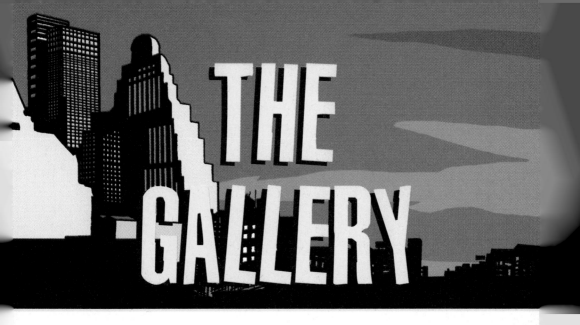

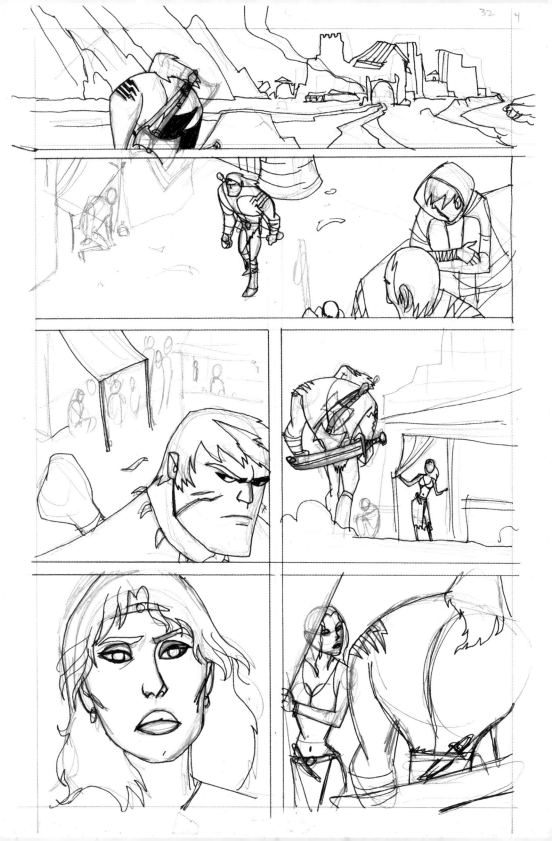

SCABBARD?

BGG

DEENA

AVON

Michael
Oeming

Zora

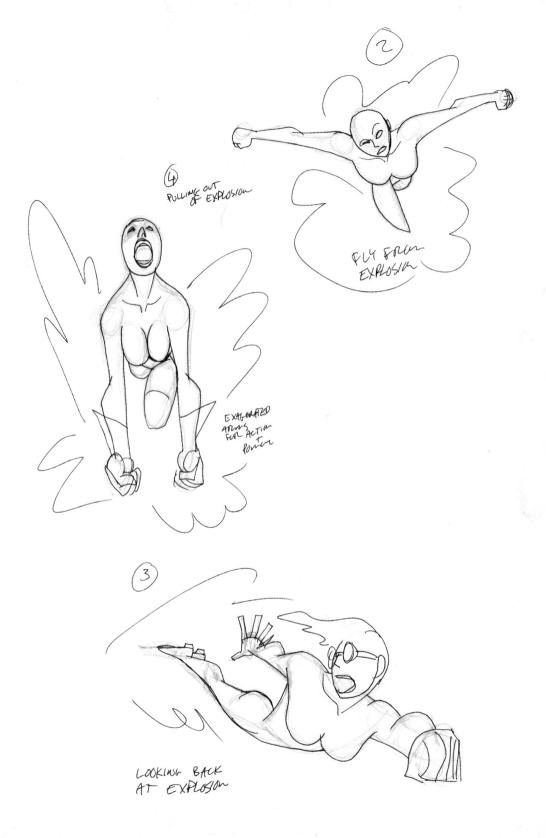

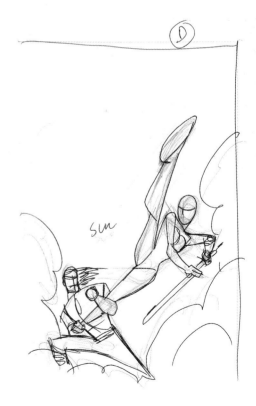

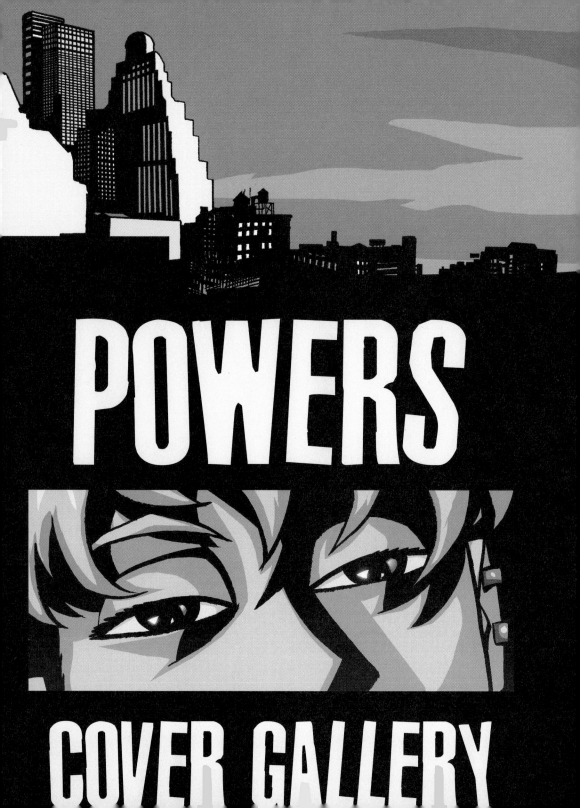

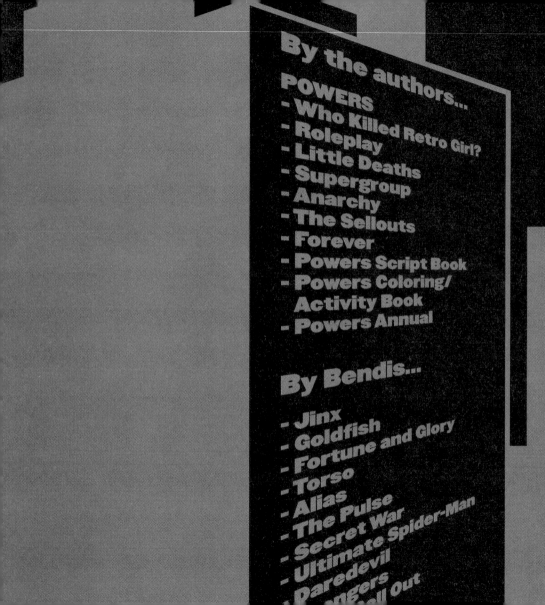